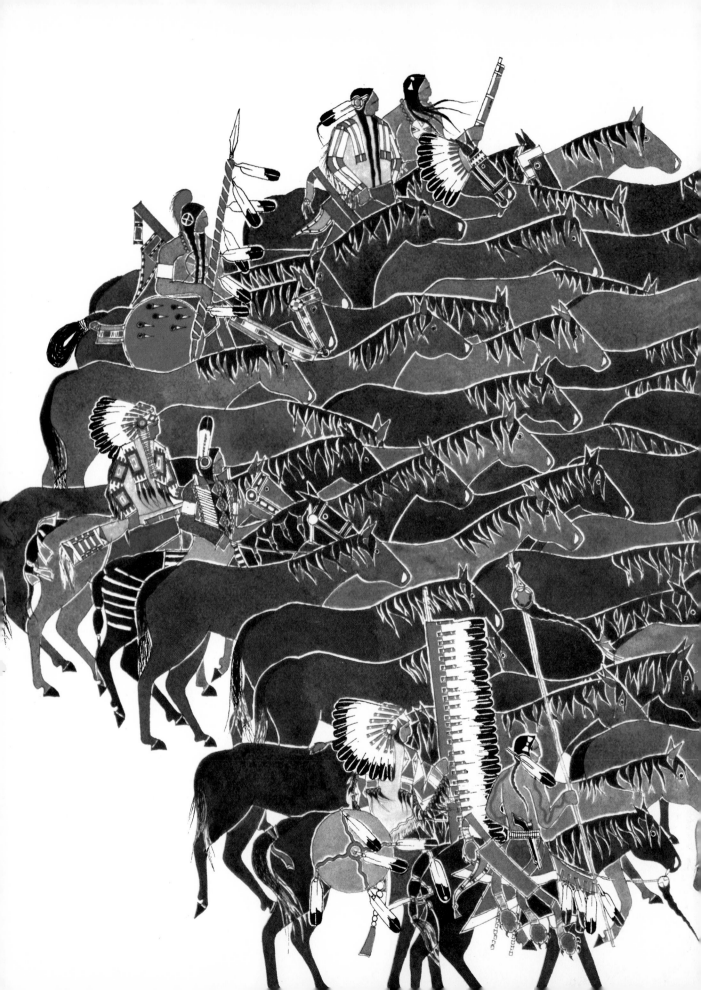

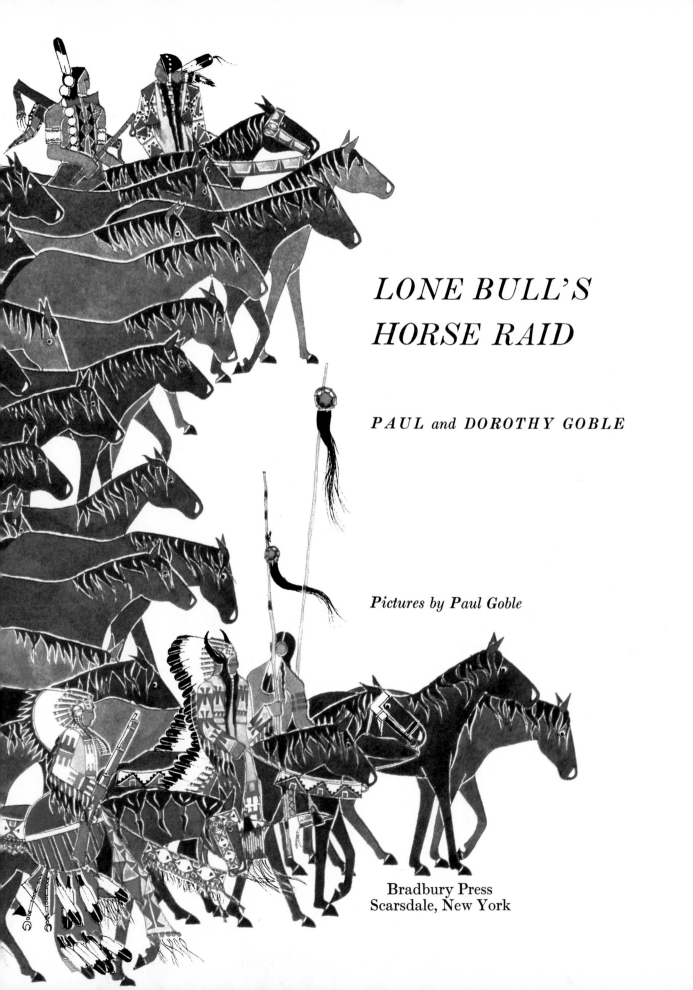

LONE BULL'S HORSE RAID

PAUL and *DOROTHY GOBLE*

Pictures by Paul Goble

Bradbury Press
Scarsdale, New York

Copyright © 1973 by Paul and
Dorothy Goble

All rights reserved. No part of this
book may be reproduced in any form
or by any means, except for the
inclusion of brief quotations in a
review, without permission in writing
from the publisher.
Library of Congress Catalog Card
Number: 73-76546
Manufactured in
the United States of America
First American edition published by
Bradbury Press, Inc., 1973
Second printing 1975

ISBN 0-87888-059-3

The text of this book is set in Scotch
Roman.
The illustrations are
paintings, reproduced in full color.

for *LAKOTA ISHNALA*

*To be alone with my war-horse teaches him
to understand me and I to understand him.
If he is to carry me in battle he must know
my heart and I must know his or we shall
never become brothers. I have been told that
the white man does not believe that the horse
has a soul. This cannot be true. I have many
times seen my horse's soul in his eyes.*

Chief Plenty Coups of the Crows

ABOUT HORSE RAIDING

The battles between the Plains Indians and the United States Cavalry have been fought so many times in novels and on the screen that today it is almost forgotten that the tribes also fought among themselves. Sitting Bull, the Sioux leader at General Custer's defeat on the Little Bighorn, is always pictured as fighting the soldiers. In reality only twenty-one of his sixty-three war honours, or "coups", were won fighting the white men; the rest were won in battles with enemy tribes.

Raiding each others' horse herds was the greatest single cause of inter-tribal wars; it gave great excitement and offered rich rewards. Horses were the Indians' only valuable property, and apart from the occasional female captive, no other plunder was sought. To steal horses from an enemy tribe was honourable, whereas stealing in the usual sense was dishonest and intolerable for a closely-knit nomadic society.

The Indians needed horses for chasing buffalo and carrying their tipis and belongings. A man with more horses than he needed was in a position to trade or lend them in return for payment or other favours. Wealth was therefore largely measured by the size of a man's herd and there are records of men who owned four or five hundred horses. These men were regarded with a mixture of admiration and contempt for hoarding. The men most admired were those repeatedly successful in capturing horses and who afterwards gave them all away to their friends; this showed they were confident of capturing more in the future, and next to bravery, generosity was the virtue most admired. As an old man, Chief White Bull of the Sioux was proud to boast of the 142 horses he had given away during his lifetime.

Children grew up in a society which held the warrior as its highest ideal, and at every step in life were encouraged to follow the example of the bravest men. A father would hold up his baby son towards the rising sun and pray: "Oh sun! Make this boy strong and brave. May he die in battle rather than from old age or sickness." Stories of raiding enemy horse herds fired young boys to imitate the warriors, and they were present at gatherings where men competed in telling and re-enacting their brave deeds. As a boy grew up he saw that only men who had proved themselves warriors were looked up to and their words heeded in the tribal councils, and later he also learned that no girl would ever look favourably on him until he had proved his bravery and won the right to wear an eagle feather.

There was fierce competition among the warriors to win personal glory. Any man could shoot and kill an enemy from a distance; it demanded little courage and received no honour. To prove his bravery a warrior deliberately exposed himself to danger by first striking an enemy with a coup-stick or bow before killing him. Such heroism won many battles against the soldiers, and after his bitter experience at the Battle of the Little Bighorn, Major Marcus Reno described the Plains Indians as "the finest light cavalry in the world".

Anyone could lead a horse raiding party, but the warriors usually followed an experienced leader who had a reputation for success. As leader he was responsible for the safety of every member and if any were lost his reputation might suffer. Parties rarely numbered more than fifteen and often there were only two or three individuals involved. They left camp quietly so that if they were unsuccessful they could return home as quietly as they had left without questions being asked. Festivities and praise were reserved for those who were successful and returned home without loss of life. Winter was the favourite season because it relieved the monotony of the long winter months. Parties left on foot or on horseback; those on foot could hide themselves and their trail more easily but were vulnerable to attack from mounted enemies. The aim of the horse raiders might be to run off some of the enemy's herds which grazed outside the camp circle, but this needed no special skill. The ideal was to creep into the enemy camp at night and take the fastest horses, the buffalo runners as they were called, which were jealously guarded and picketed outside their owners' tipis. In doing this the warrior risked losing his life and it was counted a minor war honour.

Young boys specially sought such honours because it was their first step towards recognition as brave men. They went more for the excitement and glamour than for the horses. It was their initiation into the warrior's life. On their first trip they might be expected to serve their seniors, fetching water and wood for the fire and helping in various small ways. They suffered practical jokes and teasing but were content to put up with this in return for the privilege of being members of the group. When battles were fought to regain lost horses, it was usually the boys who were in the forefront in their efforts to outdo each other. They had a reputation to make, whereas the older men had proved themselves and took fewer risks. Whether a boy distinguished himself or not on his first trip, he was from then on considered grown-up and would be invited to join one of the tribal warrior societies.

Sometimes a man went horse raiding because he had received a dream or sign of future success. A medicine man might be consulted about the interpretation of the dream and if he gave encouragement a group would soon be organised and on its way. If not, the idea was abandoned at once. Indeed at any time a member, or the whole party, might suddenly decide to return home if anyone had a foreboding of failure or death. The Indian had a unique ability to interpret both his instincts and natural surroundings. As he roamed the vastness of the prairie he read and understood every natural sign. There are many instances where a coyote's bark or the call of a crow were understood as warnings; at other times it was just a compelling presentiment of imminent danger which saved the raiders from certain death.

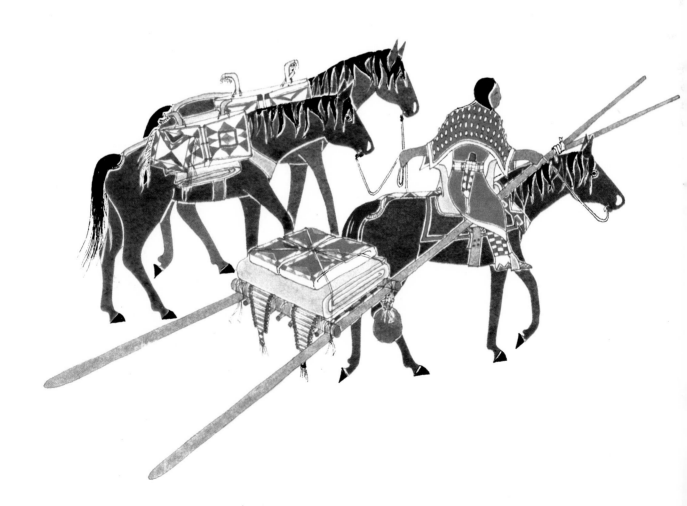

Wherever the Plains Indian went, whether horse raiding, moving camp or chasing buffalo, he put his trust in his horse. In the chase or in times of danger he expected great endurance from his mount; this was no different from what he himself was prepared to endure when the occasion demanded. He did not attribute human thoughts or feelings to his horse, nor attempt to train him in behaviour which was uncharacteristic or degrading. He recognised that his horse had a soul. He saw that the horse was an important part of the great mystery of the universe around him and therefore, like all things in nature, deserved his deepest respect. He saw horses in his dreams and visions; he sang of them in his songs and remembered them in his stories; he painted them on rocks and on his buffalo robe, his shield and on his tipi. And at the end, when death came, a man's favourite buffalo runner was killed at his grave so that he could ride the longest of all trails along the Milky Way to the Spirit World.

AUTHORS' NOTE

Horse raiding continued for several years after the Indians were hemmed in on reservations because this was the traditional way for a young man to gain a good reputation in the tribe. But the raiders were finally stopped by the White Man's law, which, instead of recognition and praise, gave a jail sentence as the only reward.

Until quite recently there were old men living on the reservations who had taken part in raids when they were young. While they were in general reluctant to speak to white men about their part in battles with the U.S. Army, for fear of punishment, they were proud to talk about their experiences in fights with other tribes. George Bird Grinnell, James Willard Schultz and others, who had lived with the Indians during the buffalo days, recorded accounts of war-parties and horse raiding.

These accounts are exciting and valuable for the insight they give into Plains Indian warfare. The accounts vary greatly in their details, but the features which are common to them all have been woven into this description of a successful horse raid. Lone Bull is a fourteen year old Oglala Sioux boy; he is a typical boy from any Plains Indian tribe about one hundred years ago. The "enemy" is the Crow tribe because at that time these two peoples considered that capturing each others' horses was a point of honour.

Surely no race of men, not even the famous Cossacks, could display more wonderful skill in feats of horsemanship than the Indian warrior on his native plains.

General G. A. Custer

Good shots, good riders and the best fighters the sun ever shone on.

General F. W. Benteen

The Sioux is a cavalry soldier from the time he has intelligence enough to ride a horse or fire a gun.

General G. Crook

The Sioux of the Northern Plains were foes far more to be dreaded than any European cavalry.

General C. King

LONE BULL'S HORSE RAID

"Be patient, my son. There is no hurry; the horses of our enemies, the Crows, will not walk away. They will be there next summer and the summer after."

My father's answer was the same whenever I asked if I could go with the warriors to capture horses.

I had already joined the men chasing buffalo and killed my first cow; I felt I was a man. I was fourteen years old and wanted to make a name for myself. I did not want to play games any more with the other boys and was tired of looking after horses around the camp. I liked best of all to listen to the stories the warriors told of battles with our enemies; I was impatient to do what they had done.

Charging Bear felt as I did and we talked about joining the first horse raiding party which left camp. We were friends, closer even than brothers, and we had agreed that if one was ever in trouble the other would always help, even if it meant one had to die.

One day in the Moon of Dark Red Cherries, July, I heard that my father was choosing men to go with him after Crow horses. It was just the chance we had been waiting for. We made up our minds to follow their trail and to join them when we were too far from home to be sent back.

My grandfather must have guessed; he knew most of my secrets and when we were beyond hearing of the tipi he said: "No man can help another to be brave, grandson, but through brave deeds you may become a great chief one day. Tomorrow when the sky begins to turn yellow, I shall be waiting over there among the trees by the creek with your horse and everything needed for your journey. Bring only your bow. Be careful; I have heard it said that the women are watching to make sure you do not run off."

It was after dark when the warriors came silently one at a time to our tipi. They did not want it known around camp that they were going out after enemy horses because many others would have wanted to go as well; a large party leaves a broad trail which is difficult to hide in the enemy's hunting grounds. My father had chosen nine warriors, reliable and experienced men who knew all about the land of the Crows. His friend Thunder Horse was there; he was a great warrior, always restless when sitting at home. When he entered the lodge father gave him the seat of honour, at the back across from the entrance.

When they were all assembled my mother placed food before them. Afterwards a pipe was filled and as it was passed from hand to hand around the circle each one smoked, asking the Great Spirit to grant him success. I can still see my father as he leaned forward to draw with a stick in the dry earth. He spoke of the trail they would take and the best points to cross the rivers and of the most likely places they would find the Crows camped at that time of year. They spoke in low voices long into the night and when the sounds in the camp grew small, the pipe was returned to the rack at the back of the fireplace. It was time to go. The warriors left quietly while my father sat for a time staring into the fire and eating a little food. Afterwards he searched for his things, my mother helping and telling him to be careful. Outside, I could hear him saddle his favourite buffalo runner. And then he was gone.

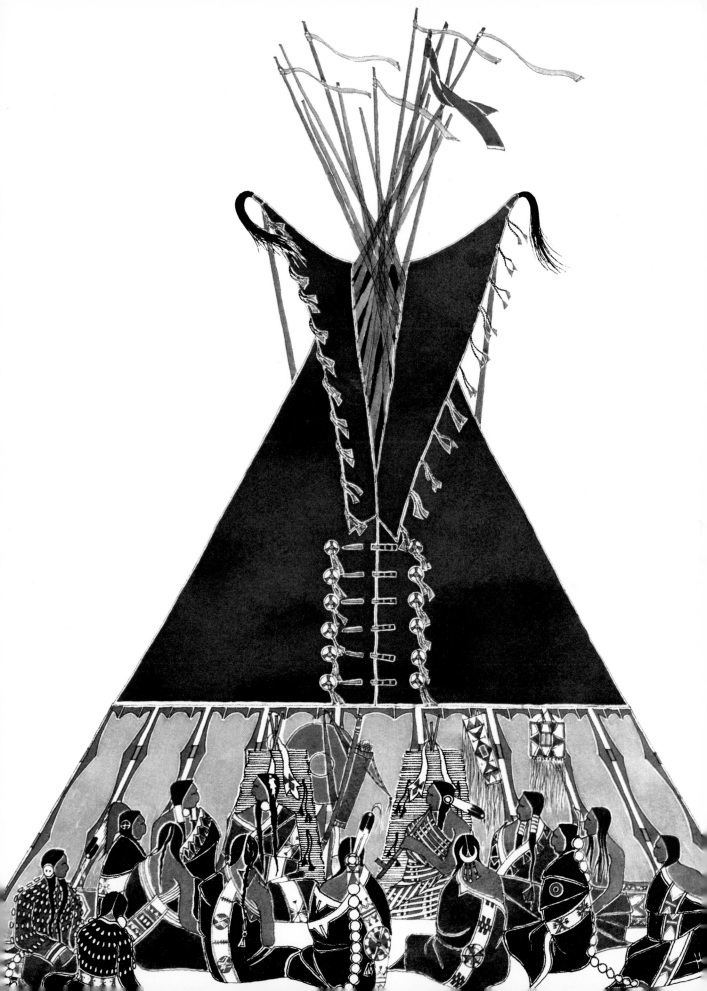

The night seemed long, waiting for the dawn. I lay on my back looking up through the smoke-hole at the stars. My mother's steady breathing soon told me she was asleep, and my little sister beside her. I was thinking how unhappy they would be and how my mother had always cried whenever I spoke about going away with the warriors. I loved her very much and did not want to make her unhappy. The flickering shadows from the fire on the tipi cover settled, and soon were gone. I was thinking about many things; listening to the murmur of the creek and the cool night breezes rustling the leaves of the cottonwood trees. How slowly the stars move . . .

Hehey! It was light when I next opened my eyes! My mother was still asleep. I took down the quiver from the pole above my head, felt under the cover for a peg, cut the thong and slipped underneath. I strode past the tipis with my blanket drawn over my face so I would not be recognised, and once beyond the edge of the camp, ran off to the creek. There stood Charging Bear and my grandfather beside him holding my horse.

"*Hau*, grandson, here you are." I was too upset to say I had slept, but he knew and said in a cheerful voice, "Your grandmother has packed everything you need in the saddlebag. Look! The sun touches the tipi poles and the women will soon be about. Go now!"

We followed the creek up into the hills and soon found the tracks where the warriors had waited for each other. The morning was bright and clear, and looking back we could see the circle of our lodges with thin wisps of smoke from the cooking-fires rising in the still air. My mother would already have missed me. Perhaps she had sent my uncle to search for me.

We travelled as fast as we could all day, sometimes losing the trail and then finding it again. When it was too dark to see we turned off the trail and hobbled our horses in some thick grass beside a stream. I was hungry. The dried meat sweetened with berries tasted good.

I rolled up in my blanket but could not sleep. It was my first night away from home and every small sound startled me; I felt like a coward. Charging Bear felt the same. We thought we would never be brave. We sat up and saw things in the dark which were not there; an owl hooted and when a coyote yelped Charging Bear thought an enemy was near. We hardly slept that night.

We set off when the sky began to turn yellow in the east, and the sun was still low over the prairie when we came to the place where the warriors had spent the night. I climbed a hill with a wide view hoping to see them, but nothing disturbed the prairie-chicken dancing to and fro among the sagebrush on every side. Far ahead an eagle circled high in the sky; perhaps he had seen our men and was waiting in the hope that they would make a kill for his morning meal. We watched him awhile, then pressed on as fast as our horses could go. Our friends were travelling fast; we did not see them that night nor the next. By then I thought we were nearing Crow hunting grounds and I began to be frightened we might never catch up with them.

Early on the fourth day we came to where they had killed an antelope and had stopped to build a fire. The ashes were still hot and the remains of their meal were scattered around. We were just enjoying some pieces and wondering why they had left so much, when riders yelling their war-cries suddenly appeared over the edge of a gulch not a stone's throw away. I grabbed my horse's reins but then realised they were our friends.

"So my son follows our trail like a coyote to eat the scraps we leave behind," my father said laughingly. "We have been watching you as the mountain lion waits for the little wolf. It was to make your heart strong. It is good that you have come. I am proud, my son. Come and eat." Later I told Charging Bear what a fright they had given me, and how glad I was that my father was not angry. We could hardly wait to reach the Crow camp.

By now we were entering Crow hunting grounds and travelled at night or in the early mornings, keeping as much as possible to ravines and low-lying places. We walked our horses so they did not tire, and when crossing high ground we waited while our scouts peeped over the top. They wore wolf-skins over their heads; it is the way of scouts to imitate the cunning wolves as they wander restlessly by night and day. We took care not to frighten the buffalo in case an enemy should see them running. During the heat of the day we hid among trees beside a river and tried to rest, but I remember the biting-flies were troublesome. We took turns to keep watch and when evening came we had a swim before setting out.

Dawn was breaking on the seventh day when we came on a broad trail where many people and horses had passed two days before. We followed it a short way along a creek when we saw riders appear over some low hills in front, coming down on the other side. There was no time to go back so we got off our horses and hid among the alders at the water's edge. I took out my bow because I thought there would be shooting. They were Crows, mostly women and young girls going to pick berries. Fortunately they had much to say to each other, for if they had looked in our direction they would surely have seen us.

As soon as they were out of sight we left the trail and climbed a high ridge where we hid in some thick pines. We stayed there while two scouts went ahead to look for the camp.

The shadows were getting long when the scouts returned, and by the time they led us to a hilltop the sun had already set. Though this happened many years ago I can still see the view as it unfolded before my eyes. Down there, about a long bowshot from us, two Crow warriors sit talking and enjoying the evening. Horses, many hundreds of them, are grazing everywhere on

the gentle slopes around them, and away down the valley beside the creek stands the circle of their tipis partly hidden among the trees and darkened shadows.

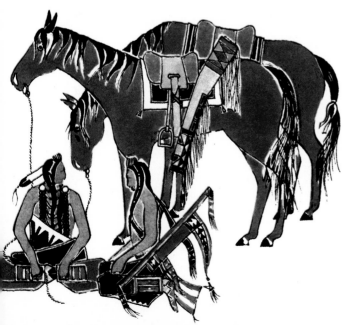

As darkness fell we lay there and watched the Crows driving their horses to the creek to drink. One by one the stars came out and the Spirits began their flickering dance of brightness in the northern sky. I was very happy; I think I was already driving horses home and could hear my grandfather singing praise-songs.

We rode down into the valley and tied up our horses in a cottonwood grove some way below the camp. I took off my leggings in order to walk quietly. Everyone made ready. Charging Bear cut cottonwood bark and we rubbed the cool sap over our bodies because horses like the sweet smell and would not be afraid of strangers in the dark. "My friends," said my father before we set off, "tomorrow the Crow women will weep for their lost horses, and their men will give chase to dry their eyes. Come what may, we are not afraid to fight. We are Oglalas! *Koya kuye*, let's go."

During our advance, we kept as close as possible to the creek where the willows were thickest. Our footsteps startled the silence of the night and I kept close to the shadow of the man in front. A sniff of smoke and cooking which drifted among the trees set my inside muttering; I wished then that I was safe at home watching my mother roasting buffalo ribs. The leaders stopped, for there, over the bushes, were the tops of the enemy tipis glowing faintly from the fires inside. We crept a little closer until we could plainly hear women's voices and a baby crying. Suddenly a dog barked, then others joined in and soon it seemed that every dog in the camp was barking. Men and women shouted to quieten them and after a while there was silence. We listened. There were footsteps in the grass ahead coming towards us. I heard Charging Bear, who was just behind me, slowly draw an arrow from his quiver. The footsteps stopped. I think I was ready to run; everyone was holding his breath, and my heart was beating like a berry-masher. Then the footsteps went back towards the camp. The Crow must have been frightened to look any closer in the stillness of the shadows, or perhaps he thought it was only a skunk which had set the dogs barking. As we waited, we heard the beat of a drum and a voice calling people to dance. This made us happy because we knew they would be too busy dancing to watch their horses.

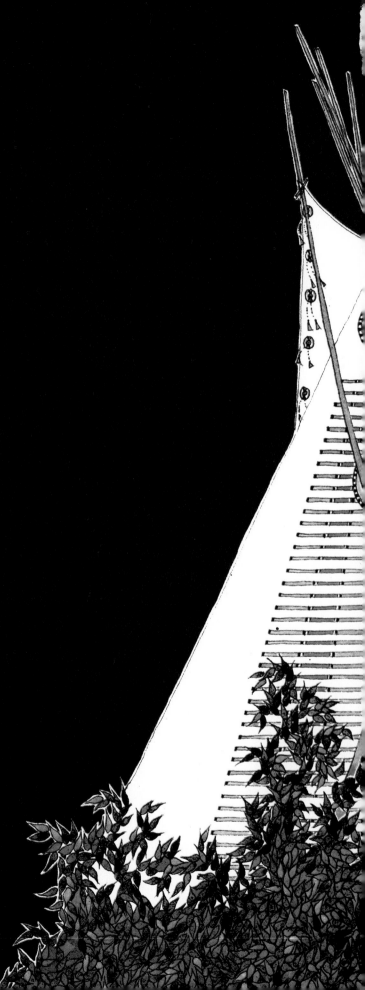

We waited, listening to the drums and
the crickets in the dark about us. The
Seven Stars were turning in the sky and I
could tell it was near the middle of the
short summer night. Most of the Crows
were already asleep; by sunrise we had to
be far away with the horses. My father
whispered that it was getting late; we
must move now or never. He told me to
keep beside him; Charging Bear went with
Thunder Horse. I think they were nervous
about us youngsters. We closed in cau-
tiously until we were between the tipis
pitched on both sides of the creek. My
father signalled me to stop and I crouched
under a cutbank beside a pathway which
the women had made going to and fro
when fetching water. After what seemed a
long time I heard the thud of hooves and
my father appeared leading two horses.
"Be careful," he whispered, "I saw a man
coming back from the dance; he went into
a lodge over there."

I was alone. I felt there were eyes watching from every side as I moved among the dark shapes of the picketed horses and enemy lodges. It was something like the game I had played so often back home, but now, at any moment, I expected to feel an arrow in my body or hear a gun go off. I can never forget the fear I felt that night. The horses had cropped the grass quite short; the ground was flat and there was nowhere to hide. Low voices came from a tipi which had the cover raised at the bottom and I could see the outlines of several people sitting around a small cooking fire. I kept to the shadows beyond the circle of light cast by the fire, and with my eyes in all directions I approached a tall painted tipi set apart a little from the rest. There was a beautiful black horse tied before the door, his body glistened like dew-covered cobwebs under the bright stars. I felt I had to have this horse, but at the same time I saw that his tether disappeared through a dark hole under the cover at the bottom of the tipi. The owner must have prized him greatly; perhaps he even slept with the tether tied around his wrist! It made me think about the story of the man who could never sleep for fear his horses would be stolen, and how he watched at night with his gun poking under the cover ready to shoot. It was too risky. I decided to try elsewhere.

Five horses were picketed outside the next lodge. The door was closed, the fire had burned out and all was still inside. The owner had not been at the dance. I approached the horses slowly and stood near them for a time so they would not be frightened. I felt for their tethers but they were tangled up. I cut one, slipped my hands along it and found it belonged to a bay with a white star on his forehead. He snorted as I approached and this made the whole bunch nervous. I listened and thought their owner would wake up, but there was no movement inside. Pressed close against the bay's warm body, and keeping him between me and the lodge, I led him slowly away. In my excitement and joy at taking my first horse I could not find the path over the bank so when I was well beyond the lodges, I gave a hoot like an owl and my father joined me.

Charging Bear and Thunder Horse soon appeared like dark shadows leading three horses. "I am going back for another," I whispered to Charging Bear. "Come with me." I wanted that beautiful black horse. My father tried to hold me back. I should have been satisfied with the one I had taken but I was young and, with Charging Bear beside me, I felt strong. I left him at the edge of camp to keep watch while I found the painted tipi.

Everything was as before; the black horse was standing where I had last seen him. I crawled quietly towards him keeping my eyes all the while on the black hole at the bottom of the lodge. The white rims of his eyes were uneasy and I could hear his tail swish restlessly. As I approached, he suddenly strode off shaking his mane and blowing sharply down his nose and then stopped abruptly at the end of his tether. Had his owner felt him pull? I knew some horses were trained to wake their owners. I kept still for a long time trying to see inside the tipi. There was no movement; I took hold of the tether, cut it, and pulling gently crawled towards him.

Just as I stood up to lead him off a shot rang out next to my ear, sending back echoes from the hills around. Quicker than it takes to tell, the Crow had pulled up the tipi cover and was running at me with a tomahawk. There was no time to think; I managed to jump on to the frightened horse, let out a loud cry and galloped off.

The camp awoke like an overturned ant-heap; men, naked except for their breech-cloths, were running from the lodges, horses were prancing at their pickets and people were shouting to one another. At the edge of camp I ran into Charging Bear. He jumped up behind me and at that instant I knew he had been shot. I shouted to him to hold on as we galloped out into the open away from the tipis.

"Hurry! Let's get away from here. Charging Bear has been shot," I was shouting as we reached the place where we had left our things. There was no time to lose; we could hear the Crows coming through the trees behind us. Charging Bear had not said a word and I knew he was in pain. I blamed myself for going back. Our warriors cracked their lariats over the crowding and rearing horses; they yelled and flapped their blankets, and the sound of hooves was like the thunder of a great herd of stampeding buffalo. With only the light of the stars to see by, I thought we had taken every horse in the camp. We worked hard to keep the herd moving; our horses stumbled down steep slopes and into ravines, splashing across rivers and slipping on loose stones. Bushes whipped my face and scratched my body; branches tore at my hair and the dust kicked up by the horses filled my eyes and mouth.

We drove them before us all night long like a dark swirling river when the snows are melting in the mountains. Some horses strayed or became tired out, but there was no time to wait for stragglers. When the first rays of the returning sun lit up the tops of the mountains behind us we stopped to wash the wound in Charging Bear's shoulder. My father tied it with a piece of buckskin tanned very soft to keep the hurt dry and clean. He now felt better and said he could ride on his own. "The sight of all our horses makes me strong," he said. We had captured very many, and among them all I had spotted my two buffalo runners.

We stopped no longer than it took to put our saddles on fresh horses. Then on again, driving them as fast as they could go, galloping awhile and then walking.

From time to time my father would turn off to one side up a small rise and look back over our trail to see if we were being followed. The trail we left was broad for we had many horses. Thunder Horse rode ahead to pick out the best trail while we followed with out-riders on both flanks to keep the herd bunched up. I stayed close to Charging Bear in case he needed help.

By the time the sun was overhead we began to hope the Crows had given up the chase. But then we saw a cloud of dust rising up into the sky way back on our trail. Everyone hurried to catch a fresh horse. The Crows would soon be upon us. There were no trees anywhere to give us cover; the land was cut by gullies leading into a dry creek with steep sides. We drove the herd down into the bottom.

"My friends," said my father, "this is a good place to hide. We will take them by surprise. I am going back with Thunder Horse to lead the Crows here. Nobody must show himself until they are right upon you. Then shoot! Fight bravely. Their horses will be tired with carrying them since daybreak."

We watched them go back along our trail and stop about the distance of a bowshot away. They got off their horses and sat down pretending to smoke. Soon we heard the sound of hooves on the dry earth. A dark spot appeared over the rise behind them, and then others followed; the next moment we could see the head and shoulders of many riders bobbing up and down over the edge. There must have been almost thirty of them in their warpaint, wearing hair-fringed shirts and eagle feathers which fluttered in the wind. What could only a few of us do against so many? A sudden dread came over me, with a feeling as of stones rolling around in my stomach.

The leading riders stopped, pointing. Then quickly taking out their weapons they charged, whipping their horses on both sides. Our friends jumped up and as they galloped away Thunder Horse's mount was shot beneath him and I thought he would be killed. My heart was with him; there was nothing I could do to help. He

turned to face the Crows singing his death-song and shooting his arrows fast, determined that more than one would die before him. But my father turned; bending low over his horse's neck he circled back right in front of the oncoming Crows and took his friend up behind him. It was a bold thing to do and I never knew how they dodged the arrows and bullets whizzing all around them. One bullet kicked up the earth at the edge of the gully where we were hiding and whined over our heads with the sound a mosquito makes by your ear. The Crows were so excited and sure of killing them that they never noticed us.

Hoka hey! Hoka hey! Charge! I was among the first to whip my horse up over the edge. I have never seen men so surprised. The Crows jerked back on their reins raising a cloud of dust. The next moment they were wheeling about, rearing and bumping into each other in their efforts to get away, leaving one of their friends on the ground, dead at our first shot. Another could not turn quickly enough and Fire Wolf swung his tomahawk, knocking him backwards out of his saddle.

The rest scattered and we were soon strung out pursuing them over the prairie. I was gaining on a Crow riding a dark bay, and in my haste dropped my arrow. He kept glancing back as he tried to reload an old muzzle-loading gun. He slipped a ball down the barrel and banged the butt on his saddle to ram it home, but as he turned to take aim my arrow knocked him forward. He let go his gun, clinging to his horse's mane, but fell when I struck him with my bow. He was young; maybe, like me, it was his first fight and if he had been a little quicker loading his gun he might have got me first. By the time I had caught his horse and found his gun, my friends had disappeared over the rise chasing the enemy. Thunder Horse, still on foot, had signalled Charging Bear to bring him a horse. "Hurry, we must get the herd started for home right away. These Crows have had enough, but others may still be coming."

Our friends soon caught us up, Spotted Elk with a scalp tied to the tip of his bow. Far in the distance the Crows watched, sitting on their horses, waiting to pick up their dead comrades. We kept on at a steady pace because we thought they might follow us, looking for a chance to get back their horses. By then Charging Bear was too tired and weak to keep in the saddle and I rode holding him in front of me for the rest of the day.

Dark thunder clouds gathered on every side as darkness fell and my father said we should stop during the storm. Charging Bear was ill; hot with fever and unable to keep his eyes open. He fell into a deep sleep as soon as we laid him down. I remember my father and Thunder Horse tending his wound by the flickering light of a small fire and saying it was nothing bad. I remember the flashes of lightning and the Thunder Beings' angry rumbling and I felt it was my fault that my friend was suffering. I remember too the gusting wind and the driving rain covering my tears which the others never saw.

When the prairie awoke next morning everything had been made new by the rain and Charging Bear was better. Even the flowers looked brighter, and the scent of sage and thirsty earth filled the air. Every little gully was covered with new earth and pools of fresh water lay in the hollows where the day before the buffalo had wallowed in the dust to keep off the flies. The Thunder Beings had taken pity on us and sent the rain to wash away all signs of our trail. We saw no more of the Crows. Our horses were scattered in every direction, grazing where they had strayed during the storm and it was near the middle of the morning before we had rounded them up.

We were almost home when we ran into an Oglala out hunting. He told us the camp had been moved down river and immediately ran off to spread the news of our return. We stopped to bathe in the river and to put on our shirts and all our best things. After combing our hair, we braided sweet-grass into it and painted our faces to show we had been successful.

Long willow sticks were cut and the three Crow scalps tied to the ends. My father gave one to me to carry saying: "Give this to a woman who mourns a relative killed by the enemy. Tell her to grieve no more, and let her hold it aloft as she leads us in the victory dance tonight."

I rode the beautiful black horse which I had taken from outside the painted tipi. He knew how excited and proud I felt. He was tall and powerful, yet gentle and eager to do everything I told him. Charging Bear rode beside me on a bay, and the wound in his shoulder had been proudly painted round with red for all to see. When the camp came in view over the willows at the bend in the river, we whipped up the herd to a hard gallop. The dogs, always alert, were the first to greet us as we charged towards the camp, shooting off our guns into the air and yelling war cries. Women left their work, children screamed with delight and men came running from the lodges to see. People were calling my name and pointing to the scalp I held as we galloped around the camp.

All about me the air was filled with the sweet smell of horses and the thunder of hooves and neighing and above it the sound of laughter and women making the tremolo. There were horses everywhere galloping and circling in a swirling dust round and round the camp; blacks, whites, bays and sorrels, proud of their beauty, prancing this way and that with their manes and tails flying like wind-driven clouds. Even the herds out on the prairie lifted their heads and neighed a welcome to the new horses. *Hetchetu whelo!*

My heart sang in my breast. How happy I was to be home! How proud as I rode beside my father to our tipi! There were tears in my mother's eyes as she greeted us. I jumped down from the black horse and put the reins into my grandfather's hands. He had helped me and in turn I wanted him to have the best horse I had brought back.

There was feasting and dancing throughout the camp for many days and nights, and to show our happiness my father invited the old and the poor to a great feast. Afterwards, when everyone was full of meat, we gave away the horses. We gave and gave until our hearts were strong with giving. It was then that I stood before them all for the first time as a warrior and told everything I had done.

In a sacred manner
I live,
To the heavens
I gaze;
In a sacred manner
I live,
My horses are many!

Stories of horse raiding and battles between the tribes will be found in these books:

BLISH, HELEN H. *A Pictographic History of the Oglala Sioux*; the drawings of Amos Bad Heart Bull. University of Nebraska Press, Lincoln, 1967.

DENSMORE, FRANCES. *Teton Sioux Music*. Government Printing Office Washington, Smithsonian Institution. B.A.E. Bulletin 61, 1918.

EWENS, JOHN C. *The Horse in Blackfoot Indian Culture*; with comparative material from other western tribes. Smithsonian Institution Press, Washington. B.A.E. Bulletin 159, 1969.

GRINNELL, GEORGE B. *Pawnee Hero Stories and Folk Tales*; with notes on the origin, customs and character of the Pawnee people. University of Nebraska Press, Lincoln, 1961.

————. *By Cheyenne Campfires*. Yale University Press, London, 1962.

————. *Blackfoot Lodge Tales*; the story of a prairie people. University of Nebraska Press, Lincoln, 1962.

————. *The Fighting Cheyennes*. University of Oklahoma Press, Norman, 1956.

HOWARD, JAMES H. *The Warrior Who Killed Custer*; the personal narrative of Chief Joseph White Bull. University of Nebraska Press, Lincoln, 1967.

LINDERMAN, FRANK B. *Plenty-Coups*; chief of the Crows. University of Nebraska Press, Lincoln, 1962.

NABAKOV, PETER. *Two Leggings*; the making of a Crow warrior. Thomas Y. Crowell Co., N.Y., 1967.

SCHULTZ, JAMES WILLARD. *Blackfeet and Buffalo*; memories of life among the Indians. University of Oklahoma Press, Norman, 1962.

SMITH, DECOST. *Red Indian Experiences*; George Allen & Unwin Ltd, London, 1949.

STANDS IN TIMBER, JOHN & LIBERTY, MARGOT. *Cheyenne Memories*. Yale University Press, London, 1967.